THE Sharey GODMOTHER

written by
Samantha
BERGER

illustrated by
Mike
CURATO

{Imprint}
MAKE YOUR MARK

New York

This is Shari T. Fairy.

She is *also* known as the Sharey Godmother.
This has nothing to do with her name, Shari.
That's just a coincidence.

It has everything to do with her love of sharing.

If you forget your lunch, Shari will share half of hers.
The bigger half.
And dessert.
And probably a snack for later.

If you want to have a party,
Shari will throw it for you.

And cook.

And decorate.

And give out gift bags.

If you need to take a vacation,
Shari will fly you there.

And share her cabana.
And her ice cream sundae.
And souvenirs.

And make you a commemorative photo album
to remember all the good times.

Shari likes to surprise people
with hot chocolate.

Or leave books
for someone else to find.

Or scoop up dog-doo
when folks forget to pick it up.

Shari loves sharing these random acts of kindness.
It feels warm and wumphy inside her heart—
like a reminder of everything good the world can be.

But some of Shari's friends wonder about her sharing.

"Isn't it *unfair* that no one else gives back as much?"
asks the Unfair-y Godmother,
who likes to point out how unfair life can be.

"Does anyone say *thank you*?"
asks the Beware-y Godmother,
who is naturally suspicious.

"Would people still be your friend
if you *didn't* share?"
asks the Scary Godmother,
who tends to ask terrifying questions.

"We're only asking because we care,"
says the Care-y Godmother,
who honestly cares.

Shari is always grateful
when her friends share their thoughts,
so she gives it a good think.

Is it *true* no one gives back as much?
Is it *true* no one says *thank you*?
And most of all . . .

Is she only sharing so people will be her friend?
This one worries her the most.

So as an experiment, Shari tries to see what *not sharing* feels like.

When it's her turn on the roller coaster,
she does not share her seat.

When she gets reggae festival tickets,
she does not bring a friend.

When she bakes her Fairy Éclair-ies,
she does not give them out like she always does.

So this is *not* sharing.

When she decides
not to refill her candy jar,
no one else fills it either.

Gradually, the candy
dwindles down and down
until there is only an empty candy jar.

Shari feels a little like an empty candy jar.

"Maybe the other fairy godmothers were right," Shari wonders.

"Not that many people *do* share equally,
and people *do* forget to say *thank you*.
Maybe I *am* giving because
I'm afraid people won't be my friend if I don't."

Yuck.

"I *told* you it was one-sided,"
says the Unfair-y Godmother.

"From now on, you can be on guard,"
says the Beware-y Godmother.

"Isn't life such a bummer sometimes?"
asks the Scary Godmother.

"Are you okay?" asks the Care-y Godmother.

Shari is not okay.

Something is wrong.

Something feels off.

Something feels all jammed up inside.

But some of Shari's *other* friends see things differently.
For them, it has nothing to do
with the *things* she shares.
It has everything to do
with the *time* she shares with them.
They can see Shari doesn't feel quite right
when she isn't sharing.

"Shari, when you share, you do it because giving makes
you feel good, not because you expect to get anything *back*,"
says the Aware-y Godmother.
She is so wise.

"When you share, you do it because generosity is in your heart,
not because you want to be *thanked* in return,"
says the Declare-y Godmother.
She always knows the right thing to say.

"Sharing is who you ARE!
You need to get out there and go be yourself!"
says the Repair-y Godmother.

Shari knows what she has to do.

Shari *bursts* through the window
and flies out into the world.

She gives her baby blanket to a mama bird building her nest—and it feels good!

She reads stories to the seniors at the senior center—and it feels great!

She sends root beer floats to a couple getting engaged—and it's the best!

By the time she refills
her candy jar, she is
100 percent back
to being herself.

Shari T. Fairy is the Sharey Godmother.
She shares because she loves to share.
She shares because it's who she is.

She shares because it feels
warm and wumphy inside her heart,
and it is a reminder
of everything good the world can be . . .

. . . and it *can* be.

For my friends: Xtine, Starla
Sunshine, Dehhhhb,
Li'l 'Cole & Yovi—
Giving Trees,
without being Stumps
—S.B.

For Nadja,
my benevolent bee
—M.C.

IMPRINT
A part of Macmillan Publishing Group, LLC
120 Broadway, New York, NY 10271

ABOUT THIS BOOK
This book was made using mixed media, including ink, paper, digital color, and photo collage.
The text was set in Kepler STD Light, and the display type is handlettered.
The book was edited by Erin Stein and designed by Natalie C. Sousa.
The production was supervised by Raymond Ernesto Colón, and the production editor was Dawn Ryan.
THE SHAREY GODMOTHER. Text copyright © 2021 by Samantha Berger. Illustrations copyright © 2021 by Mike Curato.
All rights reserved.
Printed in China by Toppan Leefung Printing Ltd., Dongguan City, Guangdong Province.

Library of Congress Cataloging-in-Publication Data

Names: Berger, Samantha, author. | Curato, Mike, illustrator.
Title: The Sharey Godmother / Samantha Berger ; illustrated by Mike Curato.
Description: First edition. | New York, NY : Imprint, 2021. | Audience: Ages 3–7. | Audience: Grades K–1. | Summary: Shari T. Fairy loves sharing so much
she is called the Sharey Godmother, but when some of her friends question whether so much sharing is good, she tries being less generous.
Identifiers: LCCN 2020019986 | ISBN 978-1-250-22230-5 (hardcover) | Subjects: CYAC: Sharing—
Fiction. | Fairy godmothers—Fiction. | Fairies—Fiction. | Conduct of life—Fiction.
Classification: LCC PZ7.B452136 Sh 2021 | DDC [E]—dc23

LC record available at https://lccn.loc.gov/2020019986

Our books may be purchased in bulk for promotional, educational, or business use. Please contact your local bookseller or the Macmillan
Corporate and Premium Sales Department at (800) 221-7945 ext. 5442 or by email at MacmillanSpecialMarkets@macmillan.com.

Imprint logo designed by Amanda Spielman

First edition, 2021

1 3 5 7 9 10 8 6 4 2

mackids.com

If this book was shared with you—
please return with care.
But if it is your very own,
find a friend and share!